Turtle and Snake
at Work

This book is dedicated
to my brother, Michael,
and to all kids
who love reptiles.

VIKING
Published by the Penguin Group
Penguin Putnam Inc., 375 Hudson Street, New York, New York 10014, U.S.A.
Penguin Books Ltd, 27 Wrights Lane, London W8 5TZ, England
Penguin Books Australia Ltd, Ringwood, Victoria, Australia
Penguin Books Canada Ltd, 10 Alcorn Avenue, Toronto, Ontario, Canada M4V 3B2
Penguin Books (N.Z.) Ltd, 182-190 Wairau Road, Auckland 10, New Zealand

Penguin Books Ltd, Registered Offices: Harmondsworth, Middlesex, England

First published in 1999 by Viking and Puffin Books, members of Penguin Putnam
Books for Young Readers.

1 3 5 7 9 10 8 6 4 2

LIBRARY OF CONGRESS CATALOGING-IN-PUBLICATION DATA:
Spohn, Kate.
Turtle and Snake at work / by Kate Spohn.   p.   cm. — (A Viking easy-to-read)
Summary: Turtle and Snake go off to work, Turtle to direct traffic
and Snake to make pizzas, and they both realize the importance
of paying attention to what they are doing.
ISBN 0-670-88258-5 (hc).—ISBN 0-14-130270-4 (pb)
[1. Turtles—Fiction. 2. Snakes—Fiction. 3. Work—Fiction.]   I. Title. II. Series.
PZ7.S7636Tu 1999 [E]—dc21 98-11595 CIP AC

Printed in Hong Kong
Set in Bookman

Viking® and Easy-to-Read® are registered trademarks of Penguin Putnam Inc.

Reading Level 1.1

Turtle and Snake at Work

By Kate Spohn

Viking

Before Work

Rise and shine!

Good morning!
Time to go to work.

Turtle's Day

Turtle has a job to do.

 He wears white gloves.

He wears a hat.

 He holds a sign.

Turtle tells the cars to go.
Go cars!

9

Turtle tells the cars to stop.
Stop cars!

Turtle tells the children to walk.
Walk children!

Turtle tells the bikes to go.
Go bikes!

Oh no, Turtle!
Look out!

Snake's Day

Snake has a job to do.

He wears an apron.

He wears a tall hat.

He holds a spoon.

To Snake
The best pizza maker!
Diva Birdy
1 slice....$1.50
small pie....$5.50
medium pie....$9.50
large pie....$12.50

FLOUR

SALT

CUP

2
1

olive oil

yeast

Snake is making pizza.
Pizza pie!
Pizza pie!

Make a ball.

Make it flat.

Throw it.

24

Spin it.
Look at that!

Pizza pie!
Pizza pie!
Spinning low.

Spinning high.

Oh no, Snake!
Look out!

After Work

The day is over.
It's time to eat.

It's been a good day after all!

Good night!
See you tomorrow.